A Gift for
YOU

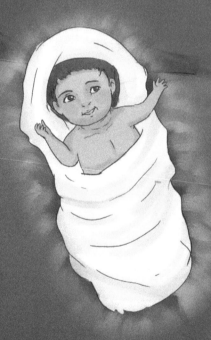

For my friends
at Holy cross!

Peace + love
through Jesus!

Ann Meuleners

ANN MEULENERS

ISBN 978-1-64079-514-3 (paperback)
ISBN 978-1-64079-516-7 (hardcover)
ISBN 978-1-64079-515-0 (digital)

Christian Faith Publishing, Inc.
832 Park Avenue
Meadville, PA 16335
www.christianfaithpublishing.com

Printed in the United States of America

This book is dedicated to my husband Bill for his encouragement and support throughout this process. I also want to acknowledge my family for their assistance and suggestions while writing my first children's book. And finally, I wish to honor the loving memory of my parents and grandparents by dedicating this book to them as well.

1

A long, long time ago God sent Me to be here by sending His special angel named Gabriel to appear.

God chose a woman named Mary, who told the angel, "Yes, I will do whatever God asks of me."

And so Mary began her journey to be my mother. Just wait and you will see!

So Mary, my mother, and her husband Joseph traveled far and wide.

Along with their donkey, you can't see me, but I was right there during that long and bumpy ride!

Somehow, I knew that my time to be born was just about to come, as that big bright star shone down on the little town of Bethlehem.

4

It was so cold and windy on that very special night.

And Mary and Joseph could not find rest any place, try as they might.

I could feel how tired my mother Mary was and knew she was no longer able.

Until, finally, a kind man helped Joseph and Mary by offering a place to rest with the animals in the stable.

So Joseph led Mary and the donkey to the stable where all the animals lay.

And it was there that I was born and placed upon a bed of warm straw and hay.

As told by the angel Gabriel, Mary and Joseph named me Jesus, their son.

For all people, I was born to spread the good news that God loves everyone!

8

When I opened my eyes, I could see my mother Mary's expression of pure joy!

And next to her I saw Joseph, who was so happy to see his baby boy!

I looked all around the barn and could smell the sweet straw, as my mother Mary wrapped me in her blanket and looked upon me with awe!

I heard the cows mooing. I saw an ox looking down.

My eyes opened wider to see all that was around.

Then I heard the birds cooing from the window up above, and even the wind was singing, as if whispering God's love.

For God was telling Mary and Joseph there was a special purpose for me—that I was born for all on this day, as a gift for each of you, do you see?

I came here to teach you that God is with you every day, and you can talk to Him and to Me, His son Jesus, whenever you wish to pray.

Now I will continue my story of how later that night some shepherds came by, and they spoke about angels that appeared in the sky!

The shepherds said a whole choir of angels sang a song of joy, telling them to go to Bethlehem and find this newborn baby boy!

The angels told the shepherds they would find me wrapped in blankets among the hay and that I would be lying in a manger, where I was born on this day.

I could hear the sheep baaing as they looked around this place, while the shepherds knelt closely by and gazed upon my face.

I smiled back at them, yet I was getting sleepy from the long day and night.

Still, Joseph, Mary, and now the shepherds, gazed down at me with delight!

As more days went by, my mother and I felt stronger after getting much needed rest, when suddenly, three kings appeared in all their glory to present us with gifts of their best!

They offered three wonderful gifts to show us their love.

And the kings told how they traveled from afar to follow a big bright star that shone up above!

Their gifts of frankincense and myrrh filled the air with a special smell as they set them down.

And I could see their gift of gold by its glimmering light all around!

Then all three kings warned us to leave very soon and listen to God's call.

For God, my Father, wanted me to grow up in another place and learn how to spread His message of love for all.

So we packed everything up, and once again my mother Mary held on to me as we rode the donkey for another long and bumpy ride!

And now Joseph led us to the town of Nazareth, where I would grow up with my family and God, my Father, always by my side.

So now whenever you celebrate Christmas and set up that tree and manger to display, remember the real reason I came here on what is called Christmas Day.

For you see, it was for each of you that I was born, as a gift for you from God, my Father, in heaven up above!

For God wants you to simply remember to take care of one another and to always show everyone your love!

ABOUT THE AUTHOR

Ann Marie Meuleners (Simon) grew up in a rural area south of St. Paul, Minnesota. She was raised in a large family of five sisters and one brother. As a child of the 1960s, Ann lived near her grandparents, aunt and uncle, and many cousins, all of whom influenced her life.

As a young girl Ann always had a love of reading, drawing, and painting. In a large Christian family, she and her siblings always looked forward to Christmas time with much anticipation. This book was inspired by the loving memory of her parents and grandparents and the gift of an antique manger that is still used today.

As a former primary and preschool teacher in both Minnesota and Wisconsin Christian-based schools, Ann decided to pursue her interest in writing her first children's book. Ann is presenting the Christmas story from a different perspective, that being as if Jesus himself is telling the story to the children.

Currently Ann lives in Eau Claire, Wisconsin, with her husband Bill of thirty-five years. She continues to paint watercolor and oil landscapes and florals, teach workshops, as well as sell prints and/or original works on the Etsy website. Ann has other ideas for children's books and hopes to continue writing and illustrating more in the future.

CPSIA information can be obtained
at www.ICGtesting.com
Printed in the USA
BVHW02*1528200818
524196BV00009B/4/P

9 781640 795167